LITTLE SIMON
Simon & Schuster Building, Rockefelle. Center
1230 Avenue of the Americas, New York, New York 10020
Copyright © 1991 by Hachette, France, and The Cousteau Society, Inc. Copyright © 1989 by
Bob Talbot (p. 16) English translation copyright © 1992 by The Cousteau Society, Inc. All
rights reserved including the right of reproduction in whole or in part in any form. Originally
published in France by Hachette Jeunesse as *DAUPHINS*. LITTLE SIMON and colophon are
trademarks of Simon & Schuster.
Manufactured in Singapore   10 9 8 7 6 5 4 3 2

Library of Congress Cataloging-in-Publication Data
Cousteau Society.   Dolphins / the Cousteau Society.   p.   cm.   Summary: An
introduction to the friendly, intelligent dolphin.   1. Dolphins — Juvenile literature.   [1.
Dolphins.]   I. Title.   QL737.C432C63   1992   599.5'3 — dc20   91-30589   CIP
ISBN: 0-671-77062-4

The Cousteau Society

DOLPHINS

LITTLE SIMON

Published by Simon & Schuster

New York   London   Toronto   Sydney   Tokyo   Singapore

THE BOTTLENOSE DOLPHIN

Mammal

Weight and size
Baby: 66 pounds, 3 feet
Adult: 440 pounds, 7-10 feet

Lifespan
Approximately 35 years

Food
Fish and squid

Reproduction
One baby every 2-3 years
12 months gestation
Nurse their young for 12-18 months.

These are dolphins,   at home in the sea.

Dolphins can leap high above the waves.

They are among the fastest swimmers in the oceans.

Dolphins are mammals, not fish. They cannot

breathe under water. Day and night, they must
swim to the surface to breathe air.

They live in groups, or pods, of many dolphins.

They protect each other and hunt fish together.

Dolphins are one of the friendliest and most

intelligent of sea creatures.

They play and whistle, leaping and diving

through the sea.